CREATURE FEATURES

More **Strange Matter**™ from
Marty M. Engle & Johnny Ray Barnes, Jr.

CREATURE FEATURES

Marty M. Engle

A
MONTAGE
PUBLICATION

Montage Publications, a Front Line Company,
San Diego, California

ISBN 1-56714-054-8

Printed in the U.S.A.

TO MOM AND DAD

THANKS FOR EVERYTHING

1

Jon almost fell asleep *despite* the screaming.

After awhile, the loud, piercing shrieks just drummed in his head, more of an annoyance than anything else.

Would she please just shut up?!

A victim's scream comes in many different styles. Some are pure vanilla, like a shallow, half-hearted wheeze. Some are musical, a perfectly sustained note, unwavering in pitch or volume. Some are inverted gasps of surprise *pretending* to be screams, like nasally air being sucked in rather than blown out.

Sometimes though, the audience gets lucky.

Sometimes they hear a deep, rich, and satisfying scream—kind of a throaty, wet scream that comes from deep inside the gut. The kind of scream that makes them feel the horror as if it was their very own. The kind that's liberating. The kind that sets their brains on fire and brings an unintentional smile to their faces.

Not so this time. Jonathan Drake and his friends had suffered through every type of scream except the last.

"OW!" Jon cried, surprised at the elbow in his ribs. "Cut it out!"

"Wake up, Jon! You're missing the best part!" Nate hissed, dribbling bits of wet popcorn from the corners of his mouth.

Jon felt his blood begin to boil. "There *is* no best part. You know *why* there is no best part? Because I've seen this movie before. I saw it when it was *Bloodinator.* I saw it when it was *B2: Blood Wars* and I saw it when it was *Bloodinator's Revenge!* And you know what, Nate? IT WAS BETTER THE FIRST THREE TIMES!"

A barrage of shushes rained down on Jon.

Thanks to his good friend, Nathan, Jon was forced to emerge from his semi-conscious state and back into the flickering nightmare that was *Bloodinator IV: Renegade.*

Jon's tired eyes were reluctantly drawn to

2

the flickering screen and to the ridiculous antics of the blood-crazed cyborg. He pulled his hand down across his face, trying to get a little feeling back.

Jon moaned. "Oh, look at this. Now he'll have a last-minute, heart-warming heart-to-heart with his soon-to-be wounded commando friend who will most certainly die in about fifteen minutes."

A type-three scream from the screen.

"Or less."

Jon shifted in his seat. "After this, he'll find out his one-time partner is really his enemy, and his girl will turn out to be working for the other side."

"Jon, please," Nate slurped.

"Finally he'll wind up hanging off either (a) a cliff, (b) a tall building, or (c) a catwalk in a warehouse that probably doesn't serve any structural purpose other than to have him *hang* off it."

"Are you trying to ruin it for us, Jon?"

"Meanwhile, the head villain, instead of getting away while he can, will wind up towering over Bloodinator, either holding a gun to his head or stepping on his fingers, or both."

3

"Point made, Jon," Nate munched, the growing exasperation in his voice clearly evident.

"At which time, The Bloodinator will say some stupid one-liner, grab the villain (incredibly moronic for being there in the first place), and throw him screaming over the side to his death."

"You finished?" Nate asked.

"Time check," Jon grumbled.

"7:45," Nate snapped.

"WHAT?! You gotta be kidding me."

Nathan slurped his Coke.

"No," Jon groaned, leaning forward and resting his head against the seat in front of him. Ah, a dirty wad of gum on the floor. At least there was something interesting to look at . . . for three hours.

Bloodinator movies were notoriously long, and lucky for him . . . this was a director's cut which *guaranteed* a gruesome, grisly surprise ending.

"That was absolutely the worst of the series!" Jon moaned, bursting through the twin doors and marching out with the rest of the weak-kneed crowd. His friends, Nathan, Albert, and Simon, strode beside him through the lobby, seven dollars lighter but with heavy hearts.

"I told you! I knew it! The ending came out of nowhere! You could tell that they put it in at the last second. Kantanka should have gotten away scott-free. There was no possible reason for him to come back and fight Bloodinator like that. NONE! That happened strictly so he could get his butt kicked by the hero."

"You're right. Of the series, this had the least amount of story and by far, the worst tacked-on ending," Albert agreed.

Albert was always quick to agree. Of the gang, he was the only other *serious* critic. Of course, he usually agreed with Jon, who could never tell if it was because Albert truly felt that way, or if he just wanted to be Jon's friend. Albert had few real friends and one too many star-geek posters on his wall. Still, he actually did have half-a-clue when it came to movies. Sometimes he could really surprise you with a keen, insightful remark.

"The effects were cool, though," Simon insisted, as usual.

Simon White. Illustrator, cartoonist,

smart-mouth extraordinaire. He always liked the visuals, especially computer visuals, but couldn't care less about content and character. He *always* paid more attention to the look instead of the story. He and Jon had a lot of similar arguments about comic books. Who was more important, the hot-shot artist or the lowly writer?

"Yeah, the effects were good," Jon countered, "but it's like Chinese food, a half-hour later you forget what you even saw!"

"Just a minute, guys," Nate said, vanishing into the boys' room.

Nate didn't care about all this stuff. To him it was just a movie, nothing more. Certainly nothing to argue about. To Nate, it was just a way for the four of them to be together and do something.

Jon couldn't think that way. Movies were too important to him. He cared about everything in them and noticed things about them that the others didn't. From the name of the cinematographer to the type of film processing they used.

Nate popped back out smiling. "Where to now, guys?"

As if he had to ask. He already knew. It

was a Friday night tradition after a lousy horror or action flick.

They had a special place to hang out and talk about it. There, they'd flush out the horrible aftertaste of *The Bloodinator IV: Renegade* with remembrances of good movies from the past.

Out on the edge of town, there's an old abandoned drive-in that's been closed for years. Since the fifties.

The Starlight Drive-In. The tall neon sign, which still towers over the road, is all broken and overgrown with vines.

So is the screen. There are big rips that flap when the wind whips through them.

The old speaker posts, yellow metal flaked with rust, line the parking field like grave markers. Some still have the speakers hanging down from their hooks like broken tentacles.

The projection booth is on the top of the concession stand. That's the creepiest place. It still has the projector.

Rumor is they tried to tear it down once, but couldn't.

According to the story, only one of the demolition guys survived. When they found him hiding in the concession stand he was curled in a ball and shaking, moaning to himself. His hair had turned snow white and he had completely lost his mind.

They never found the others, and the story the one survivor told was just too unbelievable to be true.

Or so they all thought.

2

Beneath a starry sky at the edge of town, the Starlight Drive-In sign towered over the old highway, bordering a broad, barren field. Trees and shrubs lined the dilapidated, corrugated metal fence that surrounded the lot. The lights from a few mobile homes and a convenience store were the only signs of life. Until . . .

Four bouncing headlights from four bikes raced along the highway, weaving and swerving on the embankments. Four boys riding with the kind of excitement that only comes with an empty road.

Someone had busted out the 'g' in the sign since last Friday, Jon thought. *That guy must be a real jerk. Doesn't he know this place is practically a landmark? You could see the sign half a mile away if it was all lit-up,* Jon imagined. A red neon invitation to a world of enchantment, bad food and warm summer nights.

Behind the sign, a complex, rusted metal framework held up the vast screen—or what was left of it. Vines had intertwined with the beams and cross-bracings and partially covered the Starlight Drive-In letters hanging there as well, (in case you missed the sign).

Jon, Albert, Nate, and Simon all walked their bikes up the short, overgrown driveway that led through the ticket booth. One side was marked 'Entrance'. The other marked 'Exit'. It reminded Jon of a toll booth, except for the boarded up windows and empty light sockets tracing the overhang.

"I can still *taste* that stupid movie," Jon muttered.

"It wasn't that bad," Nate countered.

"Oh, yes it was," Albert said.

"Maybe number five will be better," Simon said.

They all stopped for a moment—and groaned.

Jon felt the familiar excitement. This was

his favorite part of the trip. The part where they would stop and gaze out across the field with all the . . .

"There she is," Nate said, as they all paused, for drama's sake more than anything else.

The starry sky looked boundless, infinite, spreading over a field that swayed with blue-green grass. Yellow speaker posts jutted up from the ground and diminished with perspective, giving the parking field a wondrous sense of scale. A man-made counter to the starry display above.

The screen overlooked the field like a king over his kingdom, though a sad kingdom it was now. Barren, empty. Bare branches lay in the rows where carloads of kids used to cheer for the hero, scream at the monsters, and anticipate the coming attractions.

"Shall we?" Simon asked, bowing and waving his arm toward the concession stand.

"Benches or rooftop?" Nate asked.

"Rooftop," Albert said, looking to Jon for approval.

Jon nodded.

They all began to walk their bikes

through the rows, like a graveyard's rows, across the field toward their special place.

A small, white building, two stories tall and made of weather-beaten wood, stood at the rear of the lot, just in front of the fence.

Benches sat beside the door, in front of and under the large boarded windows, so guys getting pizza for their girlfriends could sit down and not miss anything while they waited for their drive-in cuisine.

Nowadays they served as benches for only four customers; Jon, Albert, Nate, and Simon. They only guys who seemed to *know* about this abandoned kingdom.

Or care about it.

Behind the concession stand, a small staircase led to the roof.

In the middle of that black-tarred roof was a small wooden shack.

The projection booth.

It sat all boarded and closed, its entrance door padlocked.

The only way in now was through a small, square, black window in the front. That was where the light would spring from the projector and travel an eighth of a mile to flood the screen with adventure, terror, and romance.

The roof of the concession stand used to be reserved seating for the drive-in employees and their friends.

That was where the guys would sit tonight to recall old movies and new movies they loved and hated, to debate the merits of each, to stare at the screen so far away and wonder how cool it all must have been back when the drive-in was open.

Back when it was alive.

They were about a third of the way to the concession stand when Albert said, *"Dr. Cyclops.* Now there was a movie!" The first official declaration for recollection—and debate. Albert broke an unwritten rule by bringing a movie up before everyone was properly seated, but the gauntlet had been tossed, and it was too late to call it back.

"Dr. Cyclops? 1940? Directed by Ernest B. Schoedsack? What a piece of—it was green for Pete's sake! *GREEN!"* Jon said.

It was true. The film was green. Not black-and-white like most horror pictures of the time, but dyed completely green.

"—Bright, flaming, technicolor, B-movie green. UGH! No shadows. No tension. No menace. NEXT!" Jon's call for the next feature to debate.

"I don't know, Jon. I liked the green. It was a cool special effect for its time. No one else had tried it," Simon countered.

"Of course *you'd* say that."

"Wait a sec. Besides the green, it had one of the best mad-scientists ever put on film," Albert muttered, looking at his feet as he walked.

"Excuse me. Which movie are we talking about?" Nate asked.

Jon continued, "*Devil Doll*. 1939. Same time. Directed by Todd Browning, who also directed the original *Dracula*. Same idea. Much better mad scientist."

"I don't agree."

"What? Why?"

Albert became slightly more animated, pushing his glasses up his nose. "The silver jumpsuit. The big electro-balls. The thick, round glasses and bald head. Albert Dekker is *the* stereotype wacko scientist that all others are based on."

"True, but his portrayal just wasn't

menacing enough. He *looked* the part, but he didn't *act* the part."

"WHICH ONE ARE WE TALKING ABOUT?!" Nate yelled.

"Mad scientist invents a shrinking device and uses it on unwelcome visitors," Jon explained.

Nate rolled his eyes. "From the forties? C'mon. Couldn't we talk about a more recent piece of—"

Suddenly, Nate fell silent when they felt the first quake.

Was it a tremor? The ground began to shake. To hum. Almost like someone had turned on a massive machine somewhere. They could feel the handlebars of their bikes vibrate in their hands.

"What the—" Nate asked.

"The speakers. Look at the speakers," Albert gulped.

The speaker poles were shaking and twisting in the ground. A few scattered ones near the metal fence fell over.

"W-What's going on?" Simon asked.

Jon gripped his handlebars tightly, trying

to stop the vibration. He looked from the shaking speakers to the towering sign, jutting up over the fence and behind the screen. *It was flickering.*

With a sudden burst of sparks and a snap of red neon, the sign—Starlight Drive-In—flickered to life.

"No way," Albert said.

Jon said nothing, his mouth hanging open in a mixture of awe—and dread.

The speakers began to hiss and crackle, the sound eeking through them as though it was being strained through a tin can. Fast. Mostly static, like a radio dial being turned way too fast, not stopping on any station. It grew louder by the moment, painfully loud.

A burst of light sprang from the projection stand.

The screen flickered with a moving image, blurry, undistinguishable. It sounded as if the speakers were shrieking!

The four boys turned, their hands clamped to their ears, their bikes falling to the ground.

Fearfully, they stared at the screen.

An animated popcorn box, its face smiling like a band leader's, led a procession of living, grinning snacks down a theatre aisle.

A cheery, sing-song came through speakers all over the parking field. "Let's all go to the lobby. Let's all go to the lobby. Let's all go to the lobBBBEEE! To get ourselves a treat."

"I don't like this. I don't like this at all!" Albert yelled, on the verge of panic.

"Jon, how—" Nathan began.

"We have to check this out!" Simon cried, more excited than scared.

"The projection booth," Jon said.

All four boys left their bikes there in the grassy parking field and ran all the way.

3

They never took their eyes off the cone of light cutting through the darkness over their heads as they ran across the field.

They hurried to the rear of the concession stand and stumbled up the stairs to the roof.

They paused, staring at the screen.

Bold, white type sprang up in front of a grainy cartoon illustration of the drive-in—

Please extinguish all headlights and refrain from using interior lights for the duration of the feature.

Your cooperation and patronage is appreciated!

The management

"Oh, wow. This is too bizarre!" Simon exclaimed, joining Jon.

"Over here, guys. QUICK!" Nate yelled.

He stepped back and centered himself in front of the padlocked door.

"Nate, wait! Are you sure that's a good—"

Nate yelled and flung himself against the rotted door. The clasp broke and the door flew open. Nate went tumbling inside the small shack, vanishing into the darkness with a moan.

"—idea." Jon's voice tailed off as he watched Nate's entrance.

Simon darted inside next. Jon and Albert approached cautiously, peering into the darkness.

"Nate? Simon?" Jon called.

"C'mon! You have to see this!" Simon answered from inside the room. His voice was so excited and high-pitched, it squeaked.

As Jon remembered it, the projection booth was small, dark, and usually covered in planks and old rotted paper. There were some ancient, empty film cans, yellowed posters, and the remains of the old projector, complete with the huge pipes that ran from the sides for cooling the unit. But of course, it had never worked before. Nothing could have prepared Jon for the sight—

The room looked new. The floor was clean. Swept. The movie posters that were once rotted and lying in pieces were tacked to the walls, *White Zombie* with Bela Lugosi, *Bride of the Monster, The Tingler,* all looking brand new.

The stacks of old, dented film canisters were neatly stacked and now had labels.

The thing that commanded Jon's attention, however, was in the center of the room.

The projector.

The projector that appeared to be *new.*

It was fashioned from shiny aluminum casings and duct-taped pipes. A big, round canister was in place on the top sprocket and Jon could hear it turning with a loud clicking sound.

Beside it was a metal folding chair, positioned so a seated projectionist could look out the window to the screen.

The projector was shining a beam of light out the small black window onto the giant screen—*that had no holes.*

"What's going on here?" Jon asked again. There was no reply from his friends, but he could sense their discomfort. The odd, gnawing feeling that this wasn't exactly something to be *happy* about.

As miraculous as it all appeared, Jon couldn't help but feel a growing sense of dread, a swell of horror rising in his throat and moistening his forehead.

Out the window, on the screen, on top of a swirling blob of color appeared the words . . .

Coming attractions!

4

A woman stared out from the screen, black-and-white, plain dress, generic, bee-hive hairstyle. Like a fifties housewife. Swirling snow and arctic explorers faded in behind her. Her voice sounded scared—but controlled, staged. "What waits for us in nature's no man's land?"

A man appeared in place of the woman with a slow dissolve. "Are we delving into things man was not meant to know?" he asked clinically, skeptically—daring the audience for an answer.

A third man, a scientist, appeared, although he looked more like a dentist. Glasses, gray hair. "They say it is too horrible, too fantastic, too incredible to happen. But I tell you—it could happen, could happen, could happen...

Jon watched in amazement. *It was a preview*. A preview to a coming attraction. It had to be from the fifties. Soft, black-and-white images. Big, blocky, over-dramatic type popping up all over the place, on the screen of a deserted drive-in from a projector that couldn't possibly work.

Albert leaned in beside him.

"Isn't that the preview to *The Return of the Beast?*" he asked.

Jon jerked, startled.

"Yeah. Yeah. I think it is," Jon muttered, unable to take his eyes off the screen several hundred yards away. The speakers were clear now and blaring all over the parking field. The lights along the corrugated fence had come on as well.

"Never mind the movies! Help me figure out how this thing is working!" Nate exclaimed, peering at the film strips moving along the sprockets and trailing from one spool to the other.

Simon peered at every bolt, every panel and every switch on the projector. His smile was wide and his eyes twinkled with excitement. "Maybe it knew we were coming?" Simon laughed.

"You could be right," Nate said solemnly.

Albert joined Nate and Simon as they

examined the machine, but Jon couldn't bring himself to follow suit.

He couldn't tear himself away from the window. Couldn't stop watching the images flickering across the screen.

He was watching a preview of some kind of flying-saucer-invasion movie. An invasion-from-Mars kind-of-thing. Big, hubcap-looking saucers zoomed over Washington as plain people with boring hats and ties pointed up, just slightly off their marks.

"They've come from another world to take over the Earth! And nothing on Earth can stop them!" the announcer exclaimed with all the fear and alarm of a car salesman or gameshow host.

The scene on the screen changed with an abrupt, jerky cut.

Jon watched the screen as a scientist and his pretty girlfriend, who was also the general's daughter, worked desperately in their secret desert laboratory.

It was funny, because the next movie he was going to bring up for discussion was *Invasion of the Saucer Men.* "I think I've seen this one before," Jon muttered.

The screen changed abruptly, almost as if

it sensed Jon's statement, another preview taking its place.

Jon felt his eyes water, his heart pounding faster.

"From the depths of the Amazon jungle it came. The missing link between man and fish, hidden away from time. They dared expose it to feminine beauty . . ."

On the screen, behind the blocky type of the film's title, a fishy-looking monster dragged a screaming woman from her jungle boat into the black water. The men on the boat fired a barrage of bullets at it, her scream lingering in the air.

"Stop! You'll hit the girl!" Jon mouthed the words perfectly with the gruff boat captain. Jon felt a creeping sense of dread crawling up his spine.

How was this happening? Why was this happening?

Simon, Albert, and Nate were circling the projector now, each running his hands along the metal.

"How is it getting power?" Nate wondered.

"Who loaded the film?" questioned Simon.

"Can we turn it off?" Albert asked.

Loud, hideous laughter erupted from the

speakers outside.

"Listen! Listen! Listen! DO YOU HEAR IT?! The sound of a man gone mad! An insane genius turning his back on the civilized world that scorned him."

On the screen, a wild-eyed man in a jumpsuit laughed maniacally as he reached down for a screaming girl and her boyfriend—both three inches tall.

Jon almost laughed. He couldn't believe it. A mad-scientist with a shrinking-ray, just like they were . . .

Jon shot up, fear jolting his brain.

With sudden realization, he turned his head to his friends around the projector.

Albert stood right beside the front of the projector, pushing his glasses up his nose. He peered at the beam of light for a moment. Then raised his hand—

"It knows us! It knows we're here. IT KNOWS WE'RE HERE!" Jon cried, running over—

Startled, Simon tripped over the folding chair and into the wall as Jon grabbed Albert, who shook and screamed with surprise!

Albert's hand passed through the projector's

beam. For a moment, there was a flash of pale white skin and a large dark shadow on the screen. Then a searing-white flash that enveloped the projection booth.

Simon blinked his eyes and reached out to the wall to steady himself. His head reeled and his ears were ringing. It felt like he had stood next to an explosion.

"Guys! What did—"

Simon looked around and screamed.

Though he wanted to ask his friends what just happened, he couldn't.

He was the only one standing in the projection booth.

5

Jon blinked his eyes and tried to focus. The white light felt like it was burning into his brain. He moaned as his vision cleared, and tried to stand up. It didn't feel like the wooden floor of the projection booth beneath him. It felt like—dirt or sand.

Jon looked down at his hands and yelped! "WHOA! I'm in black-and-white!"

Albert sat up with a start and blew a puff of sand from his mouth. "Uh—Where are we?"

Nate stood up and knocked the sand from his jeans and flannel shirt.

"A desert? How'd we—whoa. Why are you in black-and-white?"

Albert looked around with growing panic, the desert landscape, rocky canyons, a desolate highway—all in black-and-white. He felt the blood rush to his head in a torrent, felt his eyes flutter and his sense of equilibrium fading away.

"DON'T PASS OUT ON US, ALBERT!" Nate demanded. "Jon, where are we?"

"I don't know! The last thing I remember was Albert at the projector and—"

"Look. LOOK!" Albert screamed, pointing at the sky.

Jon saw it then, too.

Gliding straight toward them, floating over the highway, was *a flying saucer.* A hubcap-looking craft emitting a high-pitched whine that didn't quite match its movement.

"That's a—" Nate started.

"—bad special effect," Albert finished, pushing the glasses up his nose.

"JUMP!" Jon yelled.

The craft fired a white laser bolt at them! It hit the pavement where they had been standing, blowing a chunk of concrete up into the air, accompanied by an explosion that almost looked superimposed—as if it were added after the fact.

The saucer whooshed past them at terrific speed, casting a huge circular shadow on the ground.

They jumped back to their feet as it sailed

past, watching it bank and veer over the highway. The saucer's shadow didn't quite match its movements.

"Okay. That was pleasant. I think they heard you, Albert," Nate said sarcastically.

Albert's response was cut short by the rumble of vehicles—Army trucks and a Jeep—barreling down the highway in close pursuit of the alien saucer.

"The Army?" Jon asked.

It seemed surreal. *Bizarre.*

How did they get here?

The Army trucks, loaded with soldiers, continued past them, then pulled to the side of the road.

A man in a general's uniform was standing up in the Jeep before it even slowed down.

He was pointing at Jon and screaming something that could barely be made out—at least until the Jeep stopped in front of them in a cloud of dust.

"WHAT ARE YOU KIDS DOING HERE?! YOU WANT TO GET YOURSELVES KILLED? CAPTURED? CAN'T YOU SEE WE'RE—"

"Sir, look!" the soldier sitting behind the wheel said, pointing up.

The saucer banked sharply in the sky, flying back at them, *fast*.

It's wobbling, Jon thought. *Like its on a wire!*

"Fire, son! FIRE! SHOW THOSE DEVILS THEY CAN'T MESS WITH THE U.S. ARMY!"

A soldier in the back of the Jeep grabbed the large machine gun mounted behind the General's head and began firing at the approaching craft.

Jon, Nate, and Albert covered their ears as the gun roared, fire blazing out of the barrel.

The baby-faced soldier turned the gun as he fired, keeping aim on the saucer.

There aren't any cartridges flying out the side of the gun, and where is the smoke? Jon thought.

The bullets bounced harmlessly off the incoming saucer, sweeping low to the ground.

The craft fired two laser bolts and blew the two parked Army trucks to smithereens.

The soldiers sprang from the wreckage, glowing fiercely and shrieking wildly before collapsing to the ground as smoldering, glowing skeletons.

"The alien devils!" the General cursed,

31

knocking the soldier to the side and firing the machine gun himself.

The saucer flew over and past them before shooting up and fading into the sky.

The General slapped the side of the gun and squinted his piercing eyes. Jon noticed his face was way too square, too young for a general, too handsome. "Didn't even touch them. Blast. We must find a way—"

"Uh—excuse me, sir, but could—" Jon asked delicately, keeping his hands high over his head from fear of being shot.

"Sergeant!" the General barked.

"Yes sir!" the Sergeant replied, grabbing Jon's and Albert's shoulders from behind, startling them.

Where did he come from, Jon thought? *He wasn't even in the scene until . . .*

The scene?

"TAKE THESE KIDS INTO CUSTODY!"

Why? thought Jon.

"INFORM THE PENTAGON!"

Of what?

"AND GET ME PROFESSOR CHANDLER!"

Oh my . . .

Jon blinked, his mind trying to brush away the inevitable conclusion.

"WE'RE IN A MOVIE!"

"I'm telling you. We're in a movie! You! Me! All of us! This is *Invasion of the Saucer People.* I saw it three times on *Creature Features* on Friday nights."

Albert leaned in beside him, his face pleading. "Honest, Mr. General. Gee whiz. He's telling the truth—"

Jon looked over at Albert.

"Albert, please don't help."

The office was plain; simple desk, rotary-dial phone, cheap plants and a big window overlooking the Washington Monument. The General was seated with his hands folded on the neatly arranged desk. There was a blank notepad on top of a file folder, with nothing in it. A beautiful secretary was taking notes, and his trusted, unnamed aides were standing by the door.

Jon and Albert stood in front of the General's desk. Nate was sitting behind them, still staring at his black-and-white hands.

"Aren't you guys a little relaxed for a military on the brink of an invasion by a superior force?" Nathan asked.

"Typical mid-fifties invasion movie," Albert noted, looking back at Nathan, pushing his glasses up his nose.

"Hello—is anybody listening here?" Jon demanded.

"Tell me again, son. How did you and your little friends get onto the grounds of a secret military research base? What do you know of the saucer people?"

Jon peered at the General in disbelief. "What? Look. We're just kids from Fairfield Junior High out too late on a Friday night and in WAY over our heads here."

"We're—we're just trying to get home, sir," Albert said.

"There won't be much left of home, son. Of our home planet. Earth! Even now the hostile saucer forces are poised to attack any major city they want. Why even our own, Washingt—"

The secretary screamed (a type two scream) and pointed out the window as a dramatic swell of music filled their ears.

There were saucers over Washington.

7

The aides, the General, the secretary, and all the extras in the outer offices swarmed to the window and watched with audible amazement. Jon, Albert and Nate followed—*and gasped.*

A squadron of saucers was firing down upon the people and the monuments of Washington, the capital city.

Men held on to their plain hats and ties as they ran. Women with calf-length dresses shuffled along as fast as their heels would allow, even as falling chunks of concrete poured down on them from the rooftops.

Jon wasn't sure how but they were seeing everything, every attack all over the city, right from the General's window. Very convenient.

A saucer fired straight into the Lincoln Memorial, blowing Abe to kingdom-come.

37

Two saucers ganged up and fired on the National Archives Building, blowing the roof off with a sweeping attack.

"HERE COME OUR BOYS!" the General shouted with optimistic glee.

U.S. fighter planes soared in from nowhere.

Machine-gun fire from the generic fighter plane sent a saucer careening into the dome of the Capitol, exploding on impact.

Another firey barrage of gun-fire sent a saucer plowing into the Washington Monument, knocking a chunk out near the base. It looked as if a beaver had taken a bite out of it.

"Good Lord," the General said.

The monument swayed in the air a moment, then came down into the long reflecting pool with a tremendous splash, soaking hundreds of screaming tourists.

"We're doing more damage than the saucers did," Nate remarked.

The General's eyes grew steely.

"They attack the very foundations of democracy. The devils! Get Professor Chandler here, on the double!"

"Yes, sir," said a six-foot-tall aide, grabbing

his hat as he opened the office door.

"Who's Professor Chandler, sir?" Albert asked.

"Our leading scientist. He's been working on a top secret project, a way to communicate with the saucer people—and hopefully find a way to destroy them."

"That makes a lot of sense," Nate said. "Hey, wait a minute. Why would you tell a bunch of kids about a top-secret project?"

Jon shook his head anxiously, angrily. "Can we *forget* the saucer people for a moment? We need to find a way to—"

The secretary screamed again. Again a swell of music.

"Oh, great. EVERYONE to the window," Jon said, throwing his arms in the air.

The General's eyes widened. "A saucer has landed on the White House lawn! Hurry! Tell Professor Chandler we'll meet him at the saucer!" the General barked.

"Yes, sir," said a six-foot-tall aide, grabbing his hat as he opened the office door.

"Didn't he just do that?" Nate asked.

"That was another aide," Albert said.

"Oh," Nate replied.

As the General, his aides and the beautiful, if screaming-prone, secretary looked out the window, Jon pulled his friends to the side.

"All right, listen. Do either of you guys remember how we got here from the desert?"

"No. I assume they drove us here or maybe flew us in on a secret plane—hmmm. I'm not sure," Albert moaned.

"That's just it. We didn't do *anything* to get here. Get it? We just *cut* to here!"

"I don't follow," Nate said.

Jon fought the urge to scream and kept his voice low. "We simply *cut* to here. That's all! Don't you get it? We are in a movie!"

Albert and Nate looked at each other.

Neither could think of a better explanation.

"We are in *Invasion of the Saucer People!*" Jon growled.

"I want all the mobilized artillery units we can muster in place on the White House lawn now!" the General barked. "We have to be prepared to stop them! The fate of the country depends on it!"

"See? Who TALKS like that?" John exclaimed.

"WAIT!" a voice cried.

A stern but honest-looking young scientist burst into the room, carrying a strange boxy device, *like a radio*. A beautiful-but-haggard woman clung to his side.

Startled by the sudden intrusion, the General turned from the window. "Professor Chandler! Maggie!"

"Daddy!"

"General Stone. I've some shocking news regarding the saucer people. News that will change the course of the war, and—perhaps save our entire planet."

A searing laser crashed through the window, shattering it into a million fragments—striking Professor Chandler.

"RAYMOND!" Maggie shouted.

A dramatic swell of music resounded in their ears as Professor Chandler, glowing brightly, dropped screaming to his knees.

He lurched forward and grabbed Jon by the shoulders. His eyes locked onto Jon's in pure agony.

Jon screamed back into the face that was melting just inches in front of him.

Dissolving hands released Jon's shoulders. It was a skeleton that thudded to the floor.

"Raymond. Oh, no. Raymond," Maggie choked, burying her face in the General's shoulder.

Jon shook uncontrollably, a horrified scream swelling in his throat, choking him.

He looked down at the skeleton, lying at his feet and realized the seriousness of their situation. *They could die—They could die in this movie in a very real way. They had no way out.*

"Oh, man—" Nate gulped.

Albert stared, too shocked to say anything. He was trying hard not to throw up.

Trying hard not to scream.

8

A curious crowd had gathered around the saucer, held back by lines of police and National Guardsmen. Baby-faced Army soldiers crouched all around the outside perimeter of the craft, guns nervously aimed, fingers itching on the triggers.

A communications tent had been set up to the right of the craft with a large array of communications equipment—and a secret weapon.

Under the tent, a radio operator continued his radio message to the Pentagon.

"Yes, sir. The President has been notified. No, sir . . . Yes, sir. It has been confirmed. The saucer people wish to discuss the possibility of a peaceful end to the conflict—yes, sir. General Stone is going to meet with the leader personally."

Huge anti-aircraft cannons stood ready to

fire. Tank barrels poked over the heads of bazooka men and dozens of reporters tried the patience of the General, standing at the front of the crowd with three young boys, *directly in front of the saucer door.*

"Not a good place to stand," Nate said.

"What are we doing here, Jon?" Albert asked, tears welling in his eyes. "Why aren't we moving *away* from the hostile saucer? Is it just me or is this an amazingly stupid thing to do?"

"Just trust me, Albert. Right now, this is the only thing we *can* do," Jon said shakily, wringing his hands, biting his finger. If Jon was right, they were nearing the end of the movie— *and hopefully the end of this nightmare they were in.*

What else could they do? Jon thought. *Bum around with people in the movie who don't matter? Hang with non-characters? Should we run to parts of the city that don't really matter, where nothing really happens? Can we risk not being around for the climax?* The climax could very well mean their ticket home, but there was only one way to find out. *No matter how dangerous that would be.*

"Don't worry, son," General Stone said, his

hand on Albert's shoulder. "You'll be safe. I give you my personal guarantee."

"Like that professor guy?" Nate asked.

Maggie Stone, the General's beautiful daughter and finaceé to the dead Professor Chandler, moved closer to her father, forcing a brave smile.

"Just think, Dad. Thanks to Raymond's communicator, we'll be able to talk to the saucer people and bring an end to this senseless destruction. I only wish Raymond were here to—" Maggie began sobbing again, holding her hand to her mouth.

"Keep a stiff upper lip, Maggie. Thanks to your fiancée, not only will we be able to talk to these creatures—" The General shifted his eyes to the tent. "We'll also be able to take them down if necessary."

"It's opening!" Albert cried.

A door slid open on the side of the craft.

The crowd quieted. The television cameras focused in. The soldiers raised their weapons. The reporters all started their recorders and readied their cameras.

The General swelled with a deep breath and stood tall and proud. He gripped the microphone that was wired to the communications tent—and the translator.

Jon, Nate, and Albert all stared in amazement as a dim, shadowy figure appeared in the doorway.

At first it appeared human—*maybe*. The darkness inside the craft made it difficult to make out its exact shape.

"Jon, do you remember what they look like? Do you remember how this ends?" Nate asked, too afraid to breathe.

"No. Not at all. I can't focus. It feels a lot different when you're looking from *inside* the movie. I can't remember anything for certain." Jon's eyes were glued to the shadowy figure emerging from the hole in the side of the craft. His heart pounded. His pulse raced. The sweat beaded on his forehead and ran down his cheeks.

"The President of our people sends you greetings of goodwill," the General said into the microphone. The message echoed from speakers all around the area.

Nothing.

The shadowy figure didn't move. Then there was a crackle through the same speakers, then an alien voice, a low, robotic monotone.

"People of Earth. We have come—"

Everyone leaned in, anxious to hear the first words of an alien being.

"—to destroy you!"

The alien lurched from the doorway, a slimy, dripping thing, three bulgy eyes on top of a tangle of tentacles, each clutching an alien weapon.

Laser blasts erupted in all directions.

A beam struck the General directly in the face. He threw his hands up and shrieked, doubling over in crippling pain.

"I KNEW IT!" Albert yelled.

"LET'S GET OUT OF HERE!" Nate screamed.

The crowd broke in panic as the soldiers fired at the craft—to no avail.

Dozens of saucer people poured out of the opening, firing in all directions.

The laser blasts from the many-tentacled creature melted tanks, cannons, and soldiers alike. The air grew thick with smoke and human shrieks.

Then Jon stopped, under an elm tree across from the tent.

"WAIT! I REMEMBER! FOLLOW THE

GENERAL'S DAUGHTER! I THINK SHE LIVES!" he yelled, covering his head as a barrage of laser fire blew the tree to shreds.

The boys scrambled after the fleeing General's daughter, who was running toward the communication tent.

"She's going after the secret-weapon! A sonic device! The saucer people can't stand high-pitched sound!" Jon cried to Albert and Nate, running right beside him.

Then Jon tripped.

He went sprawling onto the grass.

Behind him, a hideous mass of tentacles and eyes slithered closer, training its weapons on his back.

"JON! LOOK OUT!" Nate cried.

Jon rolled to the side as the laser blasts scorched the grass beside him.

He screamed as he saw the grey mass of tentacles slithering and writhing in the air over his head. The hideous eyes stared down at him, burning with hatred.

Slime dripped down on him, onto his clothes, with a hiss. He felt his heart seize up in terror as he looked down the barrel of the alien weapon thrust into his face.

Nate and Albert screamed!

He was going to die. He could already feel the intense heat! He could already feel his flesh dripping from his bones!

He heard a hideous alien cackle.

Suddenly, the ground shook violently. ! It seemed like the whole world jerked, knocking everyone, including the aliens, off-balance.

A flash of brilliant white light and then everything went black.

In the projection booth, a frantic Simon White clutched a broomstick, staring at his friends trapped on the giant screen. Taking a deep breath, he knocked the projector in the side as hard as he could—*again.*

It barely moved.

But it was enough.

The flash left their eyes.

They sensed a great, cold darkness all around them, an eerie sense of weightlessness overcoming them.

They felt gentle waves of motion rocking them on all sides, pressing their skin, causing their hair to drift about in tangles.

Jon's eyes fluttered open and he knew immediately.

They were under water.

The water was too dark to see anything, only inky blackness in all directions.

Panic seized their minds, and desperation— *for a breath of air.*

Their lungs straining, they instinctively swam upward, at least they hoped it was upward.

Then they felt the tangles.

Something was wrapping around their arms and legs, catching about their throats. Something rough and unforgiving, scratching and tearing at their skins.

Jon, Nate, and Albert felt themselves being pulled together—then the sickening sensation of fast upward movement. The dizzying rush of water flowing past, along with a torrent of bubbles.

With a huge splash, the net came out of the water, torrents of water pouring through the bottom. It hung from the end of a crane, dangling over the side of the boat. In the mess of knotted tangles, three pale, gasping heads pressed through the net openings, screaming for help.

"What on earth—" a female voice cried.

"How the—bring it aboard!" a gruff voice called.

As the net twisted in the air, Jon tried to make out exactly where they were. He saw dense jungle foliage on all sides. Huge ferns and trees draped with vines lined the bank of a black river or narrow lake. He couldn't be sure of which. Everything was *still* in black-and-white. His heart sank, and a feeling of hopelessness kicked him in the stomach.

They were still in a movie.

But which one?

The net twisted a little more and he could make out the boat. It was a squat, weather-beaten trawler, white with black trim. A grim-looking, older man with a striped shirt held the lever to the winch. A younger, unshaven man with a white tee-shirt and a captain's hat watched grimly as they swung closer. A beautiful woman with long hair and thick lashes stood beside him, in shorts and a tied-off work shirt. Her mouth hung open in a perfect, surprised 'o'.

On the side of the boat in bold, black letters—**AMAZON EXPLORER.**

"Uh, oh—" Jon had a sneaking suspicion of where they were.

They heard the sound of a motorized winch, then a loud clanking noise. The crane moved gently, lowering the net onto the deck as the man in the striped shirt ran over to cut them free.

"Get us out of here!" Nate yelled.

"Please! You have to help us! You don't understand. We—" Albert cried.

The flash of a large, shiny blade shut him up. With a quick snap, the blade cut the rope which was pulled tightly across his face.

"Excuse me, sir! Where are we?" Jon asked.

The captain put his foot up on a wooden crate, blatantly labeled **FOSSIL-MAN EXPEDITION**, and shoved a pipe in his mouth.

"You don't know where you are? A fine thing for young fellows like yourselves to not know which part of the Amazon you're in."

The woman slid her arm under the captain's, moving up beside him. She stared with genuine concern at the boys, who were struggling to stand, drenched, cold, and miserable.

"Maybe they're spies!" the older, gruff man snarled, yanking the remains of the net off them with a jerk.

"They're just kids, Jack. They must have fallen off a passing steamer. Maybe their parents are scientists like us," she said.

"I don't know Rebecca. If that's true, maybe their parents are searching for the same thing we are—" the captain said.

Jon stared around with growing fear, hoping beyond hope that he was wrong. "W-W-What exactly are you s-searching for?"

Jack looked at Rebecca for a moment. She nodded. *Why not tell these earnest-looking young lads?* "Why, we're looking for the fossil remains of a man—half-man, half-fish, the missing link to our watery past."

Jon's breath quickened, his pulse raced, and fear clawed at his brain.

He pointed to Rebecca, "—and you were getting ready for a swim."

The woman looked surprised, then elated. "Hmm. What a great idea."

Jon screamed—and passed out cold.

10

"Jon?" The voice sounded distant, far away, almost like a dream.

"JON! WAKE UP!" Nate cried.

Jon awoke on the deck of the ship, very close to where he had passed out. The net was gone. There were more crates, some open and empty. There were large sheets spread around with thin chunks of fossilized rocks spread out in an orderly fashion on each.

Jon noticed Arnold, the gruff, older man, lying asleep in a hammock by the crane. The midday sun glared off his nearly bald head.

The captain and a tall, blond man, a research assistant, were busy putting together a steel cage.

Then Jon noticed the rope around his waist, binding his arms to his sides, and felt two squirming backs pressed against his.

"WHAT'S GOING ON HERE?!"

"Welcome back. You can thank Albert for the ropes!" Nate grumbled, struggling against his bonds.

"What?—"

"When you passed out, Albert tried to explain everything and—"

"They think we're totally insane," Jon moaned. Jon looked around frantically, tugging at the ropes. There was no way out.

Rebecca emerged from the cabin in front of them wearing a one-piece, white bathing suit with her untied work shirt over it.

"I'm sorry, kids. But it's only until we reach port later this afternoon. Then we'll find your parents or turn you over to the local authorities. In the meantime, we can't afford to risk you interfering with our important expedition." She smiled down at them as she passed, her eyes twinkling.

"Incredibly lame dialogue," Albert said, blinking back tears from his eyes. "Jon, any idea which movie we're in this time? I kinda remember this but—"

Jon gulped, thinking twice before actually

saying the name.

"*The Return of the Beast.*"

"WHAT! Isn't that the one with the—"

"Yes," Jon said miserably.

"And he slashed out with—"

"Yes," Jon replied.

"But Jon, NOBODY *lives* in that one!"

"That's right," Jon said.

"That's what I thought," Nate said.

Jon, Albert, and Nate screamed, jerking at their ropes wildly—with no success.

Fifty feet below them, cutting through the murky silt, a scaly, razor-sharp, webbed claw pushed back a curtain of seaweed.

Cold, black eyes peered up at the dark underside of the old fishing trawler.

The captain didn't even look up from his work, testing the strength of the bars, talking to his friend and research assistant, Steve. "Poor kids. Must have hit their heads when they fell off their parents' boat. Stark, raving mad—"

Steve smiled, "Well, those ropes will keep them out of trouble—"

"—*And* out of our priceless archaeological

findings," the captain said with a warm smile, waving at Rebecca, who sauntered past trailing her finger across the wooden crates.

Jon struggled vainly, watching Rebecca drop her shirt to the deck of the ship, climb to the ship's railing and flex her toes. She raised her arms high over head—*in a diver's stance*.

The black water rippled below.

Thirty feet down, scaly, webbed hands clawed at the water, rapidly ascending, approaching the vessel that dared disturb its predatory waters.

Jon felt bursts of terror race up his spine. "ARE YOU NUTS?! DON'T YOU KNOW WHAT'S DOWN THERE?!" Jon cried, straining muscles he didn't know he had.

If Rebecca hadn't turned to look at the strange young boy, *she would have seen a scaly head emerge from the water, just over the waterline, staring up at her with beady, black eyes.*

Jon could sense the impending disaster. He felt his own heartbeat thumping wildly in his chest. *It was here already.* He just knew it. Somehow, he just knew it. It was already too late.

"What do you think's down there?" she asked—the genuine fear in Jon's voice and the glazed look in his eyes giving her pause for concern.

"Something that's going to kill everyone on this lousy ship! US INCLUDED!"

Jon and Albert noticed it first. Nate was facing away.

Behind the smiling Rebecca, a pair of wide, webbed claws wrapped around the ship's railing. A hideous hiss cut through the air as it raised itself.

11

Rebecca screamed (a type two) as she turned and saw the slithering doom that was crawling onto the boat.

The beast pulled itself from the water clumsily, but with amazing speed. The gills on the sides of its head swayed and twitched with each breath. Its beady eyes glistened, and its fish-like mouth opened and closed sporadically. A loud hiss passed through the tiny, sharp teeth lining the fleshy interior of its mouth.

It had never seen a woman before. Never seen such beauty—it must have it for its own. Forever!

Jon could practically hear the announcer's voice-over as Rebecca screamed and backed away from the outstretched claws.

"RUN! RUN! REBECCA RUN!" Albert

cried. He'd always yelled directions to the stars of these horror movies before, jokingly. It was no joke now. *That thing was real.*

Deadly real.

Arnold awoke with a start, falling out of the hammock and onto the deck.

The creature grabbed Rebecca and dove over the side, plunging into the black water, clutching the terrified girl closely to its side. They vanished with a large ripple.

"BECKY!" Arnold yelled.

The captain and his assistant ran to the side of the boat, pistols drawn, firing down into the water over and over!

"WHAT ARE YOU DOING?! YOU'LL HIT THE GIRL!" Jon cried.

The bullets left a tracing line under the surface but struck nothing. The monster and the girl had vanished, leaving only a trail of bubbles, and a thin ribbon of blood.

"She's gone! Get the cage ready, Steve! FAST! I'll get the spear gun!" the captain shouted.

"Untie us! Untie us, quickly! We can help! We can—" Albert urged.

The captain darted into the cabin as the assistant hooked the crane cable to the cage.

Arnold rushed over and slipped a diving mask over Steve's head and an oxygen tank onto his back. He shoved the knife into Steve's hand.

Jon strained at the ropes until he thought his veins would burst. "We only have a few moments! He's taken her to his secret underground cave, a sunken temple at the bottom of the lagoon!"

"What then?" Nate asked.

"Then he comes back up to the boat—"

Albert gulped loudly, feeling an ice pick of terror stab his heart.

"—to kill everyone."

Steve jumped into the cage and adjusted his goggles. Arnold grabbed the crane control lever and swung the cage out over the water, lowering it rapidly as Steve gave him the thumbs up signal.

"Albert?" Jon yelled.

"Yeah?"

"Don't look—"

There was a brief calm as the cage lowered into the water. Arnold bit his lip and wiped the sweat off his chubby cheeks.

Then the attack—

The crane shook wildly, smashing into the roof of the trawler. The chain jerked and jumped as something attacked the cage below the surface with the ferocity of a shark.

They could hear a surge of bubbles and churning water by the side of the boat.

Then the cage stopped shaking and the chain went limp. A dramatic swell of music filled their ears.

"STEVE! NO!" Arnold cried, pulling the lever, raising the cage.

A twisted mesh of metal dangled off the end of the chain, the bars wrenched apart, just large enough for a man to fit through.

There was no sign of Steve.

A hideous hiss filled the air.

"LOOK! LOOK!" Jon yelled, thumping his body on the floor, trying to back away.

Two webbed claws curled around the railing at the far end of the boat. The creature was coming aboard again.

Arnold wasn't going to give it any time. He ran toward the beast, screaming. He pulled another knife from his belt, holding it high in his plump, ham-like hand.

"DON'T! WAIT!" Jon yelled.

Arnold flew into the man-like creature, stabbing and slicing at the air. The creature hissed loudly, its gills flaring out.

A webbed claw crashed into the side of the stubby man's head—cutting his screaming short, knocking him over the side with a tremendous splash.

The boys all screamed as the fish-man looked at *them* and lurched forward, *claws outstretched, swiping at the air.*

"We have to get out of here! WE HAVE TO GET OUT OF HERE NOW! IT'S GOING TO KILL US!" Jon screamed.

They all twisted and jumped about, like a living knot—*but couldn't stand up.*

The captain appeared from the cabin with the spear gun, looking with horrified eyes from the terror-struck boys floundering on the deck—to the fish-man, now lurching straight toward him!

"This is for Steve!" the captain yelled, firing the spear gun.

The creature snagged the barb out of midair. He looked at it, confused—angered.

"Can I look yet?" Albert yelled.

"NO!—CAPTAIN! LOOK OUT!"

The captain turned to run as the creature hurled the barb back at him! It struck him full in the back, knocking a shrill wheeze from his lungs.

He fell forward on the deck, right at Albert's feet. Albert opened one eye and saw the obviously fake spear sticking straight up out of the dead man's back.

"I told you not to look."

"Oh, boy," Nate said, finally able to turn around enough to see—though he wished he hadn't. *He saw a webbed, clawed foot take another step closer.*

The ropes had become loose enough to move, but not enough to get away. The boys were lying on top of each other in a tangle, watching in agony as the fish-man stepped toward them— *hissing angrily.*

Suddenly a white flash surrounded them, blinding them as they felt a tremendous jerk—

On top of the concession stand of the Starlight Drive-In, inside the small projection booth, Simon White finished stomping out the fire that had engulfed his left shoe.

He had been watching his friends about to die on the giant screen, trying to figure out how to save them, *how to get them back home!*

He had been going over every square inch of the projector, and aside from the levers on the side that shocked him with every touch, he couldn't figure out how to stop the reels from turning.

Out of sheer frustration—he kicked it. *Hard. Just as the fish-man closed in on his friends.*

It worked. The film skipped.

And though his shoe caught fire and his foot was still burning from the electrical blast, he felt relieved.

For the moment his friends were safe.

12

The light vanished faster this time, the re-orientation was less painful. Even the shock of no color was wearing off. In no time at all, Jon realized *they were in a cage.*

Like a laboratory rat cage, only human-size. The door was locked with a strange mechanism. The bars were thin but strong-looking, made of a shiny aluminum.

They were in a cage inside a lab. A very cheap-looking lab. Large metal boxes sat around the room with dials and controls that looked like parts of a car's dashboard.

Smaller cages held every kind of experimental animal possible, from spiders to rats to monkeys.

The standard beakers, tubes and wires sat on the obligatory table, along with banks of power generators—and the bizarre-looking key to the cage locks. A plain, white stool stood by the table, near the key.

"It's just like the lab from *Creature Walks Among Us,* Universal, 1956," Albert noted, pushing his glasses up his nose.

"That, my friends, was a close one," Nate said, happy to be alive. He stood up, hands on hips, and looked around the cage for any way to escape. "Where are we this time, Jon?"

"You can forget about escape, my friends." There was a pop and a skip when the man spoke, like a bad spot on a film.

"Who said that?" Albert asked.

Jon looked across the room and noticed another cage with more people! A tall, dark man in a military uniform. A balding businessman in a suit. A woman in a short black dress with short, dark, curly hair.

"Who are you?" Jon asked.

"Lieutenant Hugh Lamont, U.S. Air Force. This is millionaire investor Charles Jennings and Janet Westlake, investigative reporter for the *Times.*"

"Sounds like a well-rounded cast to me," Nate said sarcastically.

"Excuse me?" Hugh asked. His hair was perfectly combed and his eyes were piercing. He looked more like a statue or a cardboard standee than a man.

"Nothing. Pardon my friend. Where exactly are we?"

"You are unfortunate guests in the island laboratory of Dr. Zorn."

It sounded too ridiculous to be true.

"Excuse me?" Jon asked again.

"He said, the island laboratory of Dr. Xavious Zorn," an evil voice droned.

A short, stout, fireplug of a man entered the lab. He was dressed in a silver jumpsuit with many pockets. His head was bald and shiny. His eyes looked like two black dots darting around behind his thick, round glasses. A mad-scientist, if Jon had ever seen one. It was different seeing him in real life, though. Jon could *feel* the rage seething from the man as he walked by—could sense the fire that burned in his brain, the skewed, distorted view of humanity that reflected in the man's face and his expressions.

The businessman, Charles Jennings, stood and shouted angrily, "You'll never get away with this Zorn. When your other investors learn of this, they'll—"

"—Do nothing, my dear Mr. Jennings. You see, the experiment is complete. The device is fully functional."

Hugh stood beside Mr. Jennings.

"Can't you see what you're doing is wrong, Doctor? There are some things man was not meant to know!"

Again there was a crack and pop in his voice. For a moment, Jon could almost see the grainy lines whizzing past. The trademark of a really bad film.

"Your pleas fall upon deaf ears, Lieutenant. Do you take me for a fool? What nation, what government wouldn't kill to have the power I now possess?"

"What do you plan to do?" Janet asked, gripping the bars of her cage tightly.

Dr. Zorn stepped to the counter and dramatically pulled a cloth off a small pistol-looking device with an oversized barrel.

"It can't be a hairdryer. That's for sure," Nate said.

Dr. Zorn, having overheared the insolent remark, turned and glared at Nate with hate-filled eyes.

The volcano that was Dr. Zorn exploded, rattling the beakers, bottles and cages.

"ENOUGH! You dare mock ME, Doctor Xavious Zorn? You mock me as the world has mocked me. I will show you. I will show you ALL! THEY THOUGHT ME MAD! NOW THEY WILL CALL ME MASTER!"

He reached for the pistol-like device and walked over to the cage that held the others.

They backed away but there was nowhere to run. Hugh bravely stepped in front of Janet—a useless, if noble, act.

Dr. Zorn chuckled and raised the weapon, laughing as the beam of light struck them all, making them shriek in unbearable pain!

13

They all screamed as the blast surrounded them—*shrinking them down, moment by moment.*

Jon, Albert, and Nate all ran to the front of their cage and peered out, watching in horror as the three prisoners of the mad Doctor Zorn *shrank,* holding their hands up in a futile attempt to block the beam.

"It works. IT WORKS! MY DEVICE WORKS! AT LAST I WILL RULE THE WORLD!" Dr. Zorn trembled with delight, his fevered brain racing. His face twitched, dripping sweat.

Mr. Jennings, Hugh, and Janet were now the size of dolls, and shrinking even further— until they were each only three inches tall.

"I've n-never seen this one, Jon," Albert

said, his voice cracking.

"I haven't either," Jon said.

"That makes three of us," Nate said, trying to control the panic in his voice.

"Then we don't know what's going to happen. Right?" Albert asked, ready to cry. This time Jon and Nate were ready to join him.

This time, they were unprepared.

Across the room, the human victims scurried between the bars of their cage, running across the floor—across Dr. Zorn's shoes, like rats or roaches.

"YOU! My dear Mr. Jennings!" Zorn cried, reaching down and plucking the tiny businessman from the floor.

He held the poor, doll-sized man, screaming in stark terror, right in front of his face.

Zorn's face is slightly out of focus, not quite matching the crystal clear image of the screaming Mr. Jennings, thought Jon.

"You tried to turn the others against me. Called me a lunatic! Tried to get them to stop funding my experiments! You tried to crush me, Mr. Jennings."

"No! No! Please!" Mr. Jennings cried,

beating at Zorn's fingers as they closed around his lower half.

Zorn's face twisted in anger, his teeth clenched in rage. Mr. Jennings screamed as Zorn squeezed—squeezed his hand *tightly* until it made a solid fist. Mr. Jennings slumped over, draping out over the mad doctor's fingers with a dramatic swell of music.

Zorn dropped the crumpled little body, and spun around, aiming the pistol at the fleeing Hugh Lamont.

He fired—again striking the tiny Lieutenant, knocking him to the ground in a fiery blast of light.

"As for you, Lieutenant. You will experience the ultimate in death. Even now your atoms are shrinking, closing tighter and tighter! Can you feel them? CAN YOU FEEL YOURSELF SHRINKING EVEN MORE?! Your atoms will shrink, shrink, SHRINK! UNTIL YOU SHRINK OUT OF EXISTENCE ENTIRELY!" Zorn cried in delight.

"NOOOoo!" the Lieutenant screamed, clutching his head, struggling to his knees.

He shrank smaller and smaller—
Until he was no longer there.

Meanwhile, Janet Westlake, couragous reporter, had worked her way up the stool to the table top, desperate to retreive the key that would free the captive children—trapped by the insidious Dr. Zorn.

"Hurry! HURRY!" Albert cried.

Jon and Nate grabbed him away from the bars, clamping a hand over his mouth as the key tumbled from the table to floor with a clank.

The tiny reporter, Janet Westlake, scrambled back down the stool to the floor and pushed at the bizarre key with all her might, her tiny body ready to collapse from exhaustion.

Jon snapped angrily, "Be quiet Albert, you'll get his atten—"

Zorn looked around for his remaining minature captive, sneering. "And as for—"

Zorn saw her—with the key!

He rushed over as Janet gave the key a last, desperate shove. *Still too far away from the cage, too far for the boys to reach.*

Dr. Zorn grinned insanely and held his foot over Janet for a long, dramatic moment. She raised her tiny arms in protest.

"NO! PLEASE!" She screamed wildly as he brought his foot down—*crushing her flat.*

75

"NOOOO!" Jon yelled angrily.

Nate, Jon, and Albert all backed away, toward the rear of the cage.

"And as for you, my young friends—" Dr. Zorn cackled insanely.

He wiped the sweat from his forehead, licked his lips—*then fired the device into the cage.*

14

The blast hurt. Like a million hot needles piercing them all at once. They closed their eyes and threw up their hands, but it didn't help.

They began to shrink.

Jon managed to open his eyes.

He watched through the glow and blinding pain. The table tops rose, the bars of the cage grew fatter and the floor closer with each passing moment. The tiles beneath their feet seemed to be growing larger.

"T-T-he table! H-Hide under the table," Jon shouted, over the searing whine of the shrinking-ray.

Dr. Zorn stopped the beam and stepped forward, laughing loudly, anxious to snuff the life out of the rude little boys.

Nate, Jon, and Albert scrambled out between the cage bars, running as fast as they could, looking around in confusion.

"Spread out!" Nate yelled. "He can't crush us all!"

Jon looked up and saw the underside of Dr. Zorn's shoe coming down. For an instant, he saw the flash of a stained, black dress.

Janet Westlake, he thought.

He screamed and scrambled to the side, dodging the massive shoe as it crashed down behind him.

Dr. Zorn looked as though he was trying to smash an annoying bug as he tried again and again to catch Jon underfoot.

"Die, blast you. DIE!" he screamed, his face quivering, twitching, wet and cold.

Jon ran across the floor, under the table covered with equipment and smaller cages. Nate was already there, motioning with his hand for Jon to hurry.

Jon felt exhausted. The distance from the cage to the table seemed like miles and he didn't know if he could make it.

Dr. Zorn was losing it. He began alternating

between laughing maniacally and sobbing wretchedly.

The jungle fever that ravaged the brain of a genius was taking its final, dreadful toll. The would-be master of the world sank into total and complete madness.

Jon could hear the announcer's voice in his head as he ran, finally making it to Nate waiting for him in the shadows.

Just great, thought Jon. Dr. Zorn was having a nervous breakdown—and he was holding an experimental shrinking device.

"LOOK!" Nate cried.

Behind them, they saw Albert frozen in horror, just beneath the mad doctor.

"This is not a good thing!" Albert yelled in panic, waving his arms about, staring up at the weeping giant.

"ALBERT! OVER HERE!" Jon shouted.

"ALBERT! C'MON!" Nate cried.

Dr. Zorn began to stumble about, losing control of his limbs. His coordination faltered. His eyes closed for a moment and he swayed on his feet.

The device dangled, then dropped from

his open hand, hitting the floor as Albert jumped away. The weapon fired a searing, accidental blast—*at the table*.

"Uh, oh," Jon and Nate said together, staring up.

The table shrank fast, right over their heads! It was going to crush them!

They jumped away as the full-sized equipment on the shrinking table fell to the floor with thunderous crashes. Beakers. Bottles. *Cages*.

A cage hit the floor and flew open, right beside Nate and Jon. They barely managed to duck under the huge swinging door.

Nate yelled and backed away from the cage as Jon tripped and fell on his back, *screaming*.

A giant, hairy tarantula crawled out of the darkness of the cage. Its eyes stared blankly. Its mandibles dripped with slime. Its giant legs looked like hairy telephone poles as it crept across the floor, picking its way toward the fallen boy—*its prey*.

"JON!" Albert screamed, running across the floor toward him as fast as he could go. Nate shook, his eyes locked wide open, unable to move. He was numbed, mesmerized by the horrific sight.

The hairy beast scurried over the top of his friend, bouncing him around with its spindly legs. He could hear Jon screaming as the creature quickly picked him up, turned him over and brought him close to its mandibles—

Another sudden skip.

A jump. It felt as if they were rising fast on a roller coaster. Their stomachs lurched. Then another blinding light.

In the projection booth, Simon was holding on to the upper film reel with fierce determination.

His teeth were clenched and his arms felt like they were being pulled from their sockets.

He had managed to yank the reel off in the nick of time and was holding it about a foot away from the still-turning sprocket.

Electric crackles of energy flowed over his hands like fingers, shocking him, trying to pull the reel *back* onto the sprocket.

The film contiuned to unspool from the reel in his hands, curling and twisting through the air into the turning lower reel. *The movie was going to continue—no matter what.*

Finally the pain from the shocks was too

much and Simon had to let go.

The reel flew from his hand as if on a rubberband, and snapped back into place on top of the projector.

"All right. That's it," Simon moaned, shaking his burning hands.

The movie continued.

15

With a flash, the boys found themselves rising from the cold, hard—*pavement?*

"Uh—" Jon moaned, shaking his aching head. His clothes were covered in saliva and torn in several places.

People were rushing past in panicked waves, ignoring the boys who were laying on the sidewalk. *Some looked back over their shoulders, pointing excitedly.*

"Jon? JON! You're alive!" Nate cried, scrambling over, grabbing his friend.

"NATE! Oh, man. I'm alive, all right. I couldn't be hurting this much if I were dead," he said, smiling.

"JON!" Albert yelled. "I thought you were tarantula chow!" He looked at Jon with a wash of relief.

"So did I, pal. So did I! The last thing I remember was feeling those prickly hairs all over me, then I got lifted up and WHOOSH!"

"Hey—wait a minute. YOU'RE IN COLOR!" Albert yelled, pointing at Jon's red shirt. His blue jeans.

"I-I am. NO WAY! We're in color again! INCREDIBLE!" Jon shouted.

"Don't get too excited. We're still not home—yet," Nate said, putting a temporary damper on their spirits.

The crowds continued to rush past, accompanied by the distant sounds of sirens and explosions.

"Um. There's something weird about this color," Albert said, staring down at his very pale hand.

"I know what you mean," Nate said. "Your shirt is *way* too red, Jon. I mean it hurts to look at it."

Jon pulled his shirt out in front of himself and studied it for a moment, ignoring the crowds running past.

One man fell, scrambled to his feet, and kept on running, oblivious to the boys.

"Uh—Guys? I think we're in technicolor,"

Albert noted, pushing his glasses up his nose.

They stood slowly and looked around.

The streets were crowded, people running everywhere in a panic, all in one direction. Curiously, no one was in a car.

All the reds and yellows were scorchingly bright. The stoplights. The street signs. One panicked woman's yellow hat. It hurt to look at them after awhile.

"See what I mean? In the old technicolor process, all the reds and yellows looked great! *Too great.* The other colors were dull and faded by comparison," Albert explained, holding his very pale arm up in demonstration.

"So, what year would that put us in? What movie are we in now?" Nate asked.

"Jon?" Albert asked.

Jon's brain was moving a million miles a minute. *What movie? What could it be? Big city. Lots of random, generic citizens running in panic.*

Jon moved through the crowd, toward the department store window to the left. The horror-stricken crowd ran around him like river water around a rock.

He stopped and stared at a display of

televisions—a news report was already in progress, but no one was waiting around to see it.

A nervous commentator stared out of the screen with fear-filled eyes. He seemed to have been rushed on the air at the last moment and without preparation.

"—Please use caution when moving around the city. Avoid all bridges and tunnels. If possible, take shelter in basements. Take shelter in basements."

Take shelter in basements.

"Take shelter in basements," Jon muttered. *He had heard that line before.*

Albert and Nate moved up beside him.

"Help me out here, Jon. If this is technicolor, we would have to be in what, late fifties? Early sixties?" Albert asked.

"Probably. Technicolor was invented in 1932, but wasn't widely used until about 1954. Until then it was too expensive," Jon muttered.

"1964," Nate said, pointing to the license plate of a car parked at the curb.

"Right! Good! Okay. It would probably be at the tail end of the atomic monster craze. So, what would send masses of generic citizens fleeing for their lives from downtown?" Jon wondered aloud.

All three boys looked at each other, their eyes widening with dread and shocking realization.

"I-It's—" Albert stammered.

They looked up and screamed!

With a dramatic swell of music, in a jerky, surreal motion, it poked its huge head around the corner of the department store.

A giant, prehistoric reptile, fifty feet tall, with a mouth full of razor-sharp teeth and ancient lungs full of fiery, atomic breath was walking through the streets.

They all screamed at once as a flustered guy in a business suit stopped beside them, pointed up and yelled—

"GORGANTUAN!"

16

The giant lizard blinked its huge eyes and moved quickly into the middle of the intersection. The stoplight, draped on its powerline, thudded midway up his chest as he shuffled forward. People were running in all directions as it raised its head and roared—blowing a blast of atomic fire.

The fire from his mouth shot upward, reflecting in the windows of the buildings.

"HOLY—" Nate exclaimed.

"It-it really is—" Albert stammered, leaning back and staring up with a slack jaw.

"It *is* Gorgantuan!" Jon yelled.

The thundering prehistoric lizard from the past. Awakened from a million-year sleep by atomic testing at the bottom of the ocean, now seeking to reclaim the earth from mankind—

leaving a trail of destruction in his wake. Jon could hear the announcer's voice loudly, above the screaming of the crowd and the exploding powerlines.

"WHAT DO WE DO?!" Albert yelled.

Jon's body had the idea *way* before his brain caught up. "RUN!"

The boys ran down the street, blending into the terrified crowd.

Gorgantuan paused and swung his ponderous head down each street of the intersection. The sudden blast of a car horn caught his attention, and he made his decision, rapidly shuffling toward the source of the noise.

Jon paused to look back.

His movements are stiff, jerky, unnatural, both alive and not-alive at the same time, Jon thought. *Why doesn't his chest move when he breathes? Why doesn't his stomach sway as he turns?*

Gorgantuan raised his foot and smashed it down onto the car that had inadvertently blown its horn, the panic-stricken driver trapped inside.

Again and again, the beast stomped, roaring angrily. The tires blew, the hood crumpled, sending a pillar of smoke and flame high into the air.

The tiny driver inside screamed between each thunderous crash until the roof caved in completely—silencing him forever in a shower of metal and glass.

"THE ALLEY! HEAD FOR THAT ALLEY!" Jon yelled, cutting across the street.

The boys ran past a squad car as several brave police officers poured out, took aim behind their doors, and fired . . .

Catching the beast's attention.

The cops broke and ran as the beast stomped toward them, *but one was not quite fast enough.* The chunky cop screamed as the huge head bobbed down and plucked him off the pavement—his legs kicking in the air.

His partner's horrified scream rang down the streets as Jon, Nate, and Albert ducked into an alley, just down the street from the raging monster.

They nearly collapsed, nerves exhausted, minds numbed with overwhelming fear.

Desperately, they tried to catch their breaths and formulate a plan.

"Well? Any ideas?" Nate asked.

"My mind's a blank—" Albert wheezed.

Jon shook his head, his hands on his knees. "I-I can't think of anything either."

A deafening roar shook the city block.

They heard the sounds of a police helicopter flying in low, a bullhorn shouting something unintelligible.

The sounds of machine gun fire and a thunderous roar.

They looked at the entrance to the alley and watched in horrified amazement!

A flaming ball of a helicopter bounced and skidded down the street, ricocheting around like a pebble on a pond before exploding with a tremendous fireball.

Chunks of flaming debris landed in the alley, forcing them to duck their heads.

"WHOA! OKAY! Head down the alley! Quick!" Nate shouted, shoving them on.

They ran halfway before they realized the alley ended with a brick wall.

They were trapped.

"Oh, no. Oh, my—" Jon couldn't believe it. It was the worst cliché in the world and at the worst possible time.

Jon shouted angrily, "He'll find us here!

We're trapped! The timing's perfect!"

Albert screamed, pointing at the entrance of the alley.

The beast turned and peered down the alley, cocking its head to the side, ignoring the people fleeing around its massive legs. It blinked its beady eyes and roared.

"Wait a minute," Nate said. "Look how narrow this alley is! There's no way he can get his head in here! He can't reach us!"

Jon backed against the wall and prepared for the worst. "He doesn't have to."

The beast lowered its head to the entrance of the alley and took a deep breath, its chest glowing with an internal light.

With one mighty bellow, the fiery atomic breath swept down the alley.

17

Jon, Albert, and Nate all screamed, covering their heads, ready for the wall of fire to
engulf them. Waiting for the searing pain, the
roar of fire in their ears.

Instead, they felt the sensation of falling.
Then a soft impact.

They felt cool grass beneath them and
smelled sweet, night air. The sounds of crickets
filled their ears and, for a moment, everything
seemed calm.

"A-Are we dead?" Albert asked, afraid to
open his eyes.

"I don't think so," Nate said, sitting up,
also afraid to open his eyes.

Jon opened his eyes—and felt a surge of
joy, of unbridled happiness. It felt like the best

summer night in the world.

Jon looked straight up at the big, dark screen towering overhead, to the rusted old speaker posts, then all the way out to the dark concession stand. He felt the grass beneath him, patting it, making sure it was real—*then smiled.*

"Guys. We're home!"

Albert opened his eyes, unable to believe it. Could it be true?

Nate leaped to his feet and stood, staggering momentarily. A sense of overwhelming happiness rushed to his head, nearly knocking him over.

They lived. They made it back!

They looked up to the starry sky, to the dark Starlight Drive-In sign and cheered!

"We must have fallen out of the screen!" Albert shouted with joy.

"YEAH! We fell out right here! Can you believe it? I sure don't. Who is going to believe ANY of this?"

Jon shared his friends' jubilation, but couldn't shake the sense that something was still wrong. *Very wrong.*

"Simon must still be in the projection booth. Let's go. He's probably worried sick,"

Albert noted, pushing his glasses up his nose.

"I wonder if he saw any of this?" Nate asked as they started walking across the field.

In the projection booth, Simon was crouched near the floor. He was bruised, battered, and burned, but he was smiling—*hovering over a removed panel in the floor and holding an electrical cord over an empty socket.*

He had unplugged the projector.

He smirked the smirk of a warrior who had bested his worst enemy.

"Take that, you creep," he said.

Then there was a loud hum. A crackle of energy across the darkened movie screen's surface.

Jon, Nate, and Albert stopped, feeling the ground vibrate as it had before.

They turned and looked at the screen.

Their brief sense of joy and safety fled from them as they watched a leg step out of the screen to press firmly onto the grassy lot.

It was a leg about twenty feet tall, green, scaly, and very, very real.

"Oh, my—" Nate cried.

Albert swooned on his feet, nearly falling over, his mind simply refusing to believe what he was seeing.

"He followed us—" Jon muttered softly, unable to believe it himself.

With a mighty roar, Gorgantuan, The Mighty Reptile, stepped out of the screen and onto the grassy parking field of the Fairfield Starlight Drive-In.

18

The fifty-foot-tall reptile stood higher than the screen. He ducked his massive head coming through, and was now peering around, sniffing the unfamiliar air.

He noticed the unlit Starlight Drive-In sign and cocked his head to one side.

Three tiny, wildly-fleeing forms flew up the rows of speakers, their arms and legs pumping madly, leaving the reptile to ponder his new surroundings.

"HOW'D HE GET HERE?!" Nate screamed.

"THE SAME WAY WE DID!" Jon yelled back, not breaking stride.

"WHAT DO WE DO NOW?" Albert cried, holding his glasses to his face.

Simon pulled and tugged the power cord

farther and farther away from the projector, fighting the electrical fingers of energy that tried to pull it back.

"Oh, no you don't, you—"

Out the tiny square window of the projection booth, he saw a dinosaur head. *A real dinosaur head, opening and closing its massive jaws, blinking its beady eyes, and sniffing the air.*

"OH, NO!" he cried, almost releasing the power cord, but not quite. He tugged at it even harder, unable to tear his eyes away from the incredible sight outside.

Then the boys burst through the doorway.

"SIMON!" they shouted.

Startled, Simon dropped the cord.

"NO!" he shouted, grabbing for it in midair, but it was too late.

The cord snaked across the floor and plugged itself back in with a shower of sparks and a loud crack.

The projector flickered back on, projecting scenes of city destruction onto the fifty-foot-tall lizard standing in the middle of the parking field. The dinosaur turned and glared angrily at the bright, annoying light shining in its eyes.

"WAY TO GO, GUYS!" Simon screamed.

"Do you know how long it took me to get that thing unplugged?"

"It was you! You saved us when you unplugged the projector!" Jon shouted.

"Yeah! I saw you guys about to get fried so I had to think of something quick—"

"You mean you saw everything we went through?" Albert asked.

"Oh, yeah. It was amazi—"

Nate interrupted, "Excuse me, but can we look back fondly later? Right now there's a FIFTY-FOOT-TALL LIZARD ABOUT TO DESTROY US AND THEN OUR TOWN!"

Gorgantuan moved his head side to side, eyeing the strange searchlight curiously, waving its arms in front of its face to keep it out of its eyes.

Its massive tail tore speaker poles up by their concrete roots with each swing.

"We've got to do something QUICK! Or Fairfield's history!" Nate shouted.

"What do you want to do? Buy it a thirty gallon bag of popcorn and tell it to take a seat?" Albert shouted back.

Jon stared out at the tremendous beast. It

wouldn't take long for it to figure out where it was and what had happened. Then who knew what it would do? The scenes of city destruction playing across its belly didn't paint a pretty picture. It might as well have been Fairfield.

Think, Jon.

Think.

"If you guys hadn't let the projector get turned back on, we'd—" Simon yelled.

Then it hit him.

"THAT'S IT! THAT'S IT, SIMON!" Jon cried in astonishment.

"What? What's it?"

Jon took a deep breath and said, "We have to rewind the film. I'm going back in."

"WHAT?" they all shouted at once.

"ARE YOU NUTS?!" Albert yelled.

"I won't let you do it, Jon," Nate yelled.

"We have to rewind the film. Back to the mad-scientist part."

"The shrinking-ray guy? WHY? Are you crazy? He tried to kill us once! What if he succeeds this time?" Albert yelled.

"I think I understand," Nate said grimly, realizing that it could very well be the only way to save Fairfield.

Nate held the canister open, exposing the film spooled on the sprocket. Small electrical shocks made him yelp and wince in pain. "HURRY, SIMON! HURRY!" he cried.

The projector shook like a wild animal about to get tagged.

Simon grabbed the reel, still turning forward on the sprocket, and started forcing it backward, crying in pain as the projector shocked him as well. Sparks flew from the back, and blue-grey smoke drifted up from the arc-lamp housing.

"IT'S WORKING! IT'S WORKING!" Albert cried, peering intently at the images on the dinosaur spilling past onto the screen.

The images and sound moved backward as fast as Simon could turn.

"It's too slow. TOO SLOW! We'll never make it!" Albert cried.

He's right, thought Jon. There was over a mile and a half of film on that reel, all spaced to show at about 24 frames a second.

There was no way Simon would be able to rewind it fast enough.

"There has to be a switch!" Jon shouted.

Simon looked at the tiny switches jutting from a panel on the side.

"All the lettering has worn off!" he yelled.

"TRY ONE! WHAT DO WE HAVE TO LOSE?" Jon cried.

The dinosaur took a step forward, growing braver by the moment. *Perhaps it thinks there is nothing to fear in this strange new land,* thought Jon.

Simon flipped each switch in turn, each resulting in a painful shock.

He turned on a fan, turned off an automatic shutter, closed off an auxiliary sound amplifier, everything but reversing the direction of the reels.

"It's always the last one," he mumbled, skipping ahead to the last switch on the panel. Finally, the reels started turning backward, flying faster by the moment.

"YES!" Simon shouted, "That's it!"

Albert and Jon watched the images intently as the dinosaur took another step forward, then another.

"He's getting braver! We're running out of time!" Jon shouted to Simon and Nate.

The images flew back, past the

Gorgantuan rampage, past the helicopter, past the cop.

Then the island of Dr. Zorn.

"THIS IS IT! GET READY TO STOP!" Jon yelled, never taking his eyes off the flickering images.

On the screen, Dr. Zorn swayed, his hand opening, the weapon falling to the floor.

"HOLD IT RIGHT THERE!" Jon shouted, moving beside the cone of light coming from the front of the projector.

Simon released the switch.

"Wish me luck!"

Jon passed his hand in front of the flickering light—and vanished.

"Good luck, pal," Albert said, tears in his eyes. "For all our sakes."

19

On the screen (and on Gorgantuan's stomach), Albert, Simon and Nate watched the shrinking-ray strike the floor of the laboratory, firing its beam and shrinking the lab table.

This time, we aren't there, thought Albert thankfully.

Nate shuddered at the thought of the tarantula, as it crawled across the screen.

"THERE'S JON!" Albert yelled.

His full-sized friend sprinted across the lab floor, in scratchy black-and-white—*grabbing for the gun.*

Dr. Zorn stumbled back, straining to concentrate through the fever that was destroying his brain.

"What? Who are you? YOU LITTLE FOOL! DROP THAT—"

"This is for Janet Westlake."

Jon took aim and fired.

The beam struck Dr. Zorn dead-on, enveloping him completely. The mad-doctor shrieked as he collapsed to his knees, holding his head.

He began to shrink, surrounded by a poorly-animated glow.

"—The famed scientist, destroyed by the very weapon he killed to create," Jon said, in his best announcer voice.

"SIMON! HE'S SIGNALING! GET HIM OUT OF THERE! HE'S GOT THE GUN!" Albert shouted.

"NATE! NOW!" Simon cried, grabbing the reel, stopping it from turning any further. They couldn't risk anything happening to Jon now. They couldn't afford a surprise.

Nate reached down and grabbed the electrical cord, running from the projector to the floor. He touched it and screamed.

Crackles of electricity flowed around his hand, knocking him back.

"I CAN'T GRAB IT! The shocks are getting WORSE!" Nate growled.

On the screen, Jon peered out with

scared, anxious eyes, waving the gun, crying excitedly.

"Now, guys. NOW! I HAVE THE GUN! NOW!" Jon's voice echoed through speakers all over the parking field.

The dinosaur lowered its head and snarled. It started to walk faster and faster, straight toward the projection booth, roaring loudly! *It was no longer confused or afraid.*

Albert stared into the rapidly approaching jaws full of razor-sharp teeth and screamed!

"NOW! GET HIM BACK NOW!"

The jaws were nearly upon the projection booth.

"NATHAN! DO SOMETHING!" Simon shouted.

Nathan grabbed the broomstick, and with a loud yell, shoved it under the power cord—popping it free.

20

Jon fell out of the screen, tumbling to the ground with a soft thud, the shrinking-ray in his shaky hands.

In the projection booth three boys and a projector stared out of a tiny square window. A set of enormous jaws lunged down, tearing off a section of the roof.

They looked up at the roaring beast and screamed!

The projector cord snaked through the air like a whip and plugged itself back in.

Jon scrambled to his feet, taking aim at the massive, scaly tail swinging through the air in front of the concession stand.

"Chew on this!" he shouted—firing the

shrinking-ray.

The beam arced through the air, striking Gorgantuan solidly in the back.

The guys in the projection booth all ducked as the terrifying head swung away.

The Mighty Reptile shrieked loudly and turned around angrily, surrounded by the glow of the beam.

He crouched low and started running straight at the shooter, *mouth open, thirsty for the young boy's blood.*

He was about twenty-feet-tall when he left the concession stand, roaring loudly and bellowing fire.

Three-feet-tall by the time he got half-way to Jon, not noticing the speaker posts that were now level with his head.

It was a lizard barely an inch tall that ran up to Jon and attacked his sneaker, gnawing savagely at the rubber toe.

Jon kicked him away with a smile and waved at the cheering boys in the projection booth across the parking field.

"He did it. HE DID IT!" Albert cheered.

"YES!" Simon cried.

Nate waved excitedly at his friend. The friend who had saved his life—and the entire town of Fairfield.

Jon looked up at the scenes of total destruction still playing out on the screen above him and smiled even wider.

That wouldn't be Fairfield.

At least not tonight.

He brought the barrel of the weapon up to his mouth and blew across the tip, making a hollow whistle as he had seen done in so many B-movies.

He pushed the device into his pocket and started moseying on back toward the concession stand.

After all, there was still the matter of a haunted projector.

Albert and Nate were still cheering, and Simon was sighing with relief, running his fingers through his hair when he noticed the projector started running a little faster, shaking a little harder than it was before.

In fact, he started to back away from it,

smelling a strong odor, like an electrical burn.

"What? What's going on?"

Albert and Nate stopped cheering and stared at the projector as it shook violently, like a freight train was driving through it.

The reels spun so fast they started to smoke. The arc-lamp in its housing flared brightly, as bright as the sun.

"Oh, no. OH, NO! LOOK!" Albert cried, pointing across the field, past the sauntering Jonathan Drake—to the screen.

The screen started flickering faster with images, fleeting glimpses of monsters from at least a dozen horror movies—probably more.

Jon hadn't notice it yet, but they did.

Everyone in the booth saw the monsters coming out of the screen.

21

Movie monsters of every size and description poured down from the screen.

From savage, rubbery fish-creatures to jerky animated skeletons, to cheesy man-sized leech-men. The very icons and images that youthful nightmares are made from. The creatures that served to inspire screams and dreams of fun and excitement. *Now in the real world. Now inspiring very real, violent terror.*

All of them, over a hundred, rose from the grass in front of the flickering screen, some hissing, some roaring, some screeching—all with one thing on their simplistic, matinee minds.

Kill the boy.

"Melting-men, Blood-leeches. Wasp-women. Oh, man. He doesn't see them! HE

DOESN'T SEE THEM! JON! LOOK OUT! LOOK OUT BEHIND YOU!" Albert shouted.

Jon continued to walk toward the concession stand and his waiting friends. He was staring at the ground and whistling, one hand on the shrinking device, the other swinging by his side. He was a hero. *A hero.*

He heard something and looked up.

What? What was Albert trying to tell him? He couldn't quite make it out.

Something about monsters?

What was he . . .

Jon turned and nearly fainted. All the fear he had ever felt welled up at once and made him stagger backward, stumbling toward the concession stand.

A wall of movie monsters was sweeping toward him, stalking him across the overgrown field.

Their eyes glowed. Their fangs glistened. Their claws clacked and sliced at the cool night air.

Jonathan Drake realized he was about to be destroyed by every creature he had ever fallen in love with at the movies.

He ran faster than he thought possible, flying across the field toward the waiting concession stand.

"STOP IT! STOP THE PROJECTOR! PULL THE PLUG!" Albert yelled.

A field of crackling energy surrounded the trembling device. Nate pulled his hand back, howling in pain when he tried for the plug again. "AAH! NO WAY! It's not going to work!"

Simon grabbed the folding chair and yelled, slinging it high over his head and bringing it down on top of the projector with a loud CRASH! It didn't even make a dent. The reels continued to turn, even faster than before.

The movie continued to roll.

Jon flew into the room and slammed the door behind him!

"DID YOU SEE THEM? THEY'RE RIGHT BEHIND ME! QUICK! GIVE ME SOMETHING TO BRACE THE DOOR WITH! ANYTHING! HURRY!" His eyes darted about wildly, his breath coming out in raspy wheezes.

Nate grabbed the folding chair from the floor and ran over to help Jon. They braced the chair against the door and held it fast.

"That's not going to work!" Albert cried. "They're too strong! They're going to break in here and they're going to kill us!"

"Stop the stupid projector! Simon, stop the stupid projector!" Jon yelled.

"I can't! We can't get near it! The electrical field is too much now!"

The first pounding started.

A low, resounding thud, heavy against the door. Then another. And another.

With each blow the door cracked a little more. The chair slid a bit further. Nate and Jon started to cry, white bolts of terror traveling up and down their spines, jolting their brains with the realization that they were about to die for real—*and it was no movie.*

22

The pounding grew more fierce.

The cracks in the door grew wider.

Outside, they could hear an assortment of howls, whines, growls, and hisses.

The sounds of monsters moving past one another, jockeying for the best position.

"We can't keep them out much longer!" Nate shouted, pushing back as the door pushed in.

"I know! I KNOW!" Jon cried in return.

He dug his shoes into the floor and pressed his back against the door with all his might. "I'm thinking!"

Simon had grabbed the broom handle and was furiously smashing it down onto the projector again and again—but each blow bounced off harmlessly. The electrical bursts springing from the projector's insides acted like a shield.

"I wish they'd just get it over with! I just wish this could all be over!" Albert screamed, closing his hands over his ears, trying to drown out the slurping, wet noises coming from behind the door.

Then it hit Jon.

Albert had the answer!

He looked up from the door. "What did you say, Albert? QUICK! WHAT DID YOU SAY?!"

"I said I wish this could all be over."

Jon's face lit up. "That's it! How long were we in the movie? In the screen?"

"I don't know, a c-couple of h-hours, I guess," Albert stammered, hunkering down into the far corner.

"Would you say the same, Nate?"

Nate pushed hard against the door, grimacing. "Yeah. I guess that's about right. Time flies when you're having fun!"

"SIMON! Can you see the film reel? The top one! How much is left?" Jon shouted.

"I can't see it! I have no idea!"

Jon thought a moment.

"It doesn't matter! All we have to do is hang on for a few more seconds!" Jon yelled.

A hairy, clawed hand burst through the door, grabbing Nate by the arm.

Nate screamed and backed away, tugging his arm from its grasp.

"NO! Nate! Hang in there! HELP ME!" Jon yelled, trying to hold the door—*but it was too late.*

The door splintered, collapsing around him like a wave.

An ocean of bizarre monsters stared in at them. They stepped forward slowly, dramatically, milking the terror for all it was worth.

Jon and the others backed away, toward Albert who was trembling in the corner, too terrified to open his eyes.

"A-All w-we have to do is make it a few seconds more. A few seconds," Jon shouted, his heart threatening to burst.

The monsters flooded into the room, one after another, their claws outstretched, their mouths opening, their eyes gleaming.

Simon swung his broomstick at a few of the creatures at the front of the pack. They grabbed it effortlessly and tossed it aside.

"Just a few more seconds," Jon moaned.

They could feel the first claws touch them,

gliding across their skin—could feel the hot breath from their hideous faces, sensed the finality of the moment—the imminence of death!

The monsters faded for a moment.

Their images skipped and jumped, like they were on a bad film strip.

Jon couldn't believe his eyes.

He was right.

The monsters returned strong again, terrifyingly close, but then blinked—and faded out completely.

There was a clacking noise coming from the projector.

The end of a film strip smacking itself over and over and over . . .

The projector died with a soft whine and a dimming light.

23

Four exhausted, but exhilarated, young men gripped the handlebars of their bikes and began walking down the remains of a devastated drive-in parking field.

The sky above them was shining bright with stars, in stark contrast to the dark Starlight Drive-In sign towering over the dilapidated metal fence.

"Okay. So how did you know?" Albert asked. "How did you know the monsters would just—end?"

"It was what you said. You wished it would be over. We were in a feature, Albert. *A creature feature.* Like most features, it ran about two hours long," Jon said, staring at the ground as he walked.

Albert still looked perplexed. "Okay, but

how did you know the two hours were just about up? We couldn't see the reel."

"You've seen a lot of movies, Albert. Could there have been a better possible place to end it? See what I mean? Like all good suspense movie, the heroes were saved in the nick of time," Jon said.

"Pretty cool there, Jon," Nate remarked.

"Excellent special effects, I must say," Simon said.

Albert started to laugh, "But Jon—what if it had been a director's cut?"

They all stopped and looked at Albert, then began to laugh. They all laughed hard and loud, thrilled to still be alive and under such a beautiful, starry sky.

Jon, Simon, Nate, and Albert all walked past the ticket booth, not looking up at the sign that was flickering back to life.

They didn't notice the crackle of the speakers or hear the whine of a projector starting up.

A cone of light sprang from the projection room, sailed across the desolate field and hit the silver screen.

No one counted on a double feature.

About the Authors

Marty M. Engle and **Johnny Ray Barnes Jr.**, graduates of the Art Institute of Atlanta, are the creators, writers, designers and illustrators of the **Strange Matter**™ series and the **Strange Matter**™ World Wide Web page.

Their interests and expertise range from state of the art 3-D computer graphics and interactive multi-media, to books and scripts (television and motion picture).

Marty lives in La Jolla, California with his wife Jana and twin terror pets, Polly and Oreo.

Johnny Ray lives in Tierrasanta, California and spends every free moment with his fiancée, Meredith.

And now
an exciting preview
of the next

STRANGE MATTER™

#16 The Weird, Weird West

by Johnny Ray Barnes Jr.

Sundown.

Standing alone in the middle of the dirt street, I watched the horizon. Shimmering waves of heat rippled over the ground, bathed in a hazy, orange glow.

Something is about to happen.

Pounds of skin-burning dirt blew past me, obscuring my view of the ball of fire in the sky as it said farewell for the day.

So did I.

Laughter. A toothless old man, his face hidden under a matted, gray, spit-covered beard, eyes squeezed into glossy black marbles, rocked in a chair on a storefront porch to my left. The old codger carried on as though he'd seen this a million times before, and knew I had no chance at all.

Shut up, old man.

Glimpses of others. By-standers standing

by the side the road, nothing but shadows in the thick blanket of dirt. I heard more laughter. I heard well wishes. But I didn't hear anyone offer to help.

Sweat glazed my hands, making them feel heavy and clumsy. My throat was so dry it made swallowing too painful to contemplate. But my eyes stayed clear, focused on the end of the street. Waiting.

Then he came.

Lumbering through the sheet of dust like a curtain opening, the gunman came forth.

Lit from behind by the setting sun, I saw only saw a black outline of the man who wanted to kill me—a terrifying silhouette.

Tall. Gangly. Moving with a creep rather than a walk. He seemed slow. No. Not slow. Precise. He took large, formidable steps. He came closer. Revealing more. He wore tattered rags and a rotted Stetson that stayed affixed to his head, defying the wind.

Closer.

There were parts of him that didn't make sense. Parts I could see through. Parts that looked like exposed bone. Pieces hanging from where they shouldn't be. The sun shone *through* him. I didn't want him coming any closer.

He stopped.

He held his hands over his guns. Ready.

Over his guns . . .

Jutting from the holsters at his sides. Two guns. Two bullets. *For me.*

The wind died. The sun dimmed. The old man stopped laughing.

I heard a voice.

"Draw."

Options tore through my mind.

Talk it out or run, but do not draw.

Do not draw.

DO NOT DRAW.

My hands wouldn't listen. Reaching for my six shooters, I came up empty. *My holsters were empty!*

I heard explosions from the other end of the street.

I felt something strike my chest—*suddenly my legs were no good.*

I dropped to the ground.

Everything went black.

"Rise and shine, Shane."

Along with Pop's voice came the sound of my blinds being drawn. Sunlight invaded my dark sanctuary and I groaned at its intrusion.

"Get up, son. I've got news."

"School's cancelled? We're taking summer vacation early this year?" I yawned hopefully, opening my eyes to see Pop standing over me, waiting to make sure I was awake.

"There's been an earthquake," he announced.

"An earthquake? Here? In Fairfield? And I slept right through it?" I'd never forgive myself.

"Not here. In Mullinfield. Quite high on the Richter scale, too. Benjamin Lewis called me this morning. His home's been hit pretty hard." Pop fixed the collar on his golf shirt . . . *golf shirt*? No suit? No tie?

"Aren't you going to work today?" I asked.

Pop winked, grinning slightly. "That's what I wanted to tell you. As his insurance agent, Benjamin wants me to take a look at the damage. Your mother and I are driving up there today. We'll probably stay the weekend."

No way.

I shot up, wide awake and itching to see the destruction. "I WANT TO SEE THE EARTHQUAKE! You're taking me, too. Right?"

"You've got school today, m'boy," Pop's voice took on a serious tone, "your grades haven't been so hot. Letting you miss school for any reason right now probably isn't a good idea. You're staying here with Grandpa."

GRANDPA?

Of all the torturous . . . they can't do this to me. Not for three days. Not seventy-two hours of bad stories, false teeth, pasty food, and whistled snoring. Not Grandpa. Not the woes of pain, the game show participation, or the rolled cigarette smoking. *Gag, the smoking.*

"Please, Dad," I begged. "Let me come with you. I'll study hard when I get back. I'll make you proud."

"It's a done deal, son. Grandpa's already here, and we're ready to go." Pop slapped me lightly on the knee, punctuating the end of our conversation.

I hopped out of bed and followed him as he left the room. Mom's hand patted my back as she passed me in the hall.

"You be good and don't give your grandfather any trouble, okay?" She hung her purse over her shoulder, then remembered something. She reached into it and pulled out fifteen dollars. "This is for the weekend. Don't spend it all at the arcade. And please be good." A kiss on the cheek, then, "*Oh,* hi Dad."

"Hi, Ellen," a smothered voice strained from the LazyBoy, then it got slightly excited. *"HEY SHANE-BOY!* We're gonna be roommates, son!"

"Hey, Grandpa," I said, my hopes for viewing the earthquake aftermath dying at the sight of him.

Grandpa sat in a wrinkled heap in the chair, a tribute to the fringes of mortality. White hair, big bushy eyebrows, spotted brown leather skin with a turkey-gobbler throat. He wore a sweater, and a cap that read 'Good Day Tires'. It had been on his head since before I was born. He always steadied himself on his cane, even while watching television, as he was doing just before we walked in. What was on? *The Weather Channel.* Very loud.

"Boy, you're not going to wear your P.J.'s to school are ye? Those little girls won't know what to think . . ." He laughed silently, bouncing up and down but not making any noise.

Grandpa humor. I wanted to tell him that things had changed a lot since his school days on the prairie. I could wear a kilt to school and no one would look twice. But I decided to chuckle it off instead.

Mom and Pop added a few more things to the List of Things For Me To Do, then bade us *adios.*

"Take care of the house, son," Pop said. "And don't worry. I'll get lots of pictures." He had to. It was his job.

"And don't let Grandpa fall asleep with one of those rotten cigarettes in his mouth. He'll burn himself up!" Mom warned in a whisper.

After a hundred "no problems", Grandpa and I finally convinced them their house would be in good hands, though in Grandpa's case, nervous, old shaky ones. After that, my parents sped off, leaving Grandpa and me to stare at the road in silence for a long moment afterwards.

I looked forward to their return.

I got ready for school quickly. A splash of water on my face, a squirt of toothpaste in my mouth, and even some of Pop's cologne behind my ears. Then, as an afterthought, I decided to leave on my plaid pajama top. Just for Grandpa.

I cruised into the den, heading for the door before Grandpa could stop me with one of his stories. That's when I heard the whistling snore. Looking carefully over at the LazyBoy, I saw my elder's head slumped forward, sawing major logs.

Asleep already.

Suddenly he shot back in the seat, eyes still

closed, and started to moan.

"MOTLEEEE ... CLAYTON MOTLEY ..."

A name. He cried it out four more times. He was having a nightmare. It sounded like a terrible one.

My skin crawled as I suddenly remembered my own dark dream. Before I awoke, I wanted to cry out just like Grandpa.

". . . CLAYTON MOTLEY . . ."

Every time he said the name, my heart pumped faster. My veins twisted. My breathing became shallow. I saw the dark silhouette again, felt the bullets crash into my chest.

Who was he?

Who was Clayton Motley?

And did I want to find out . . . ?

132

There goes the neighborhood.

STRANGE FORCES

The invasion of Fairfield begins

May 96'

WHAT CAN YOU DO ON THE STRANGEMATTER™ WORLD WIDE WEB PAGE?

WHAT CAN'T YOU DO?!

CHECK IT OUT!

- Communicate with other Fan Fiends! Find a pen-pal or share a story!
- **Talk with the authors of Strange Matter™!** Ask a question! Voice your opinion, straight to the guys who write the books!
- Check out the very latest books with full-color 3-D illustrations you can't get anywhere else!
- Download and read sample chapters from any of the books in the Strange Matter™ library—right on your computer!
- Explore the outer reaches of science-fiction and horror with the all-new MISSING LINKS!
- Catch up on Strange Matter™ news with STRANGERS™ the on-line newsletter.
- Find out about the special surprises and contests coming soon!

http://www.strangematter.com

STRANGE MATTER™

Order now or take this page to your local bookstore!

☐	1-56714-036-X	#1 No Substitutions	$3.50
☐	1-56714-037-8	#2 The Midnight Game	$3.50
☐	1-56714-038-6	#3 Driven to Death	$3.50
☐	1-56714-039-4	#4 A Place to Hide	$3.50
☐	1-56714-040-8	#5 The Last One In	$3.50
☐	1-56714-041-6	#6 Bad Circuits	$3.50
☐	1-56714-042-4	#7 Fly the Unfriendly Skies	$3.50
☐	1-56714-043-2	#8 Frozen Dinners	$3.50
☐	1-56714-044-0	#9 Deadly Delivery	$3.50
☐	1-56714-045-9	#10 Knightmare	$3.50
☐	1-56714-046-7	#11 Something Rotten	$3.50
☐	1-56714-047-5	#12 Dead On Its Tracks	$3.50
☐	1-56714-052-1	#13 Toy Trouble	$3.50
☐	1-56714-053-x	#14 Plant People	$3.50
☐	1-56714-054-8	#15 Creature Features	$3.50

I'M A STRANGE MATTER™ ZOMBIE

Please send me the books I have checked above. I am enclosing $_____ (please add $2.00 to cover shipping and handling). Send check or money order to Montage Publications, 9808 Waples Street, San Diego, California 92121 - no cash or C.O.D.'s please.

NAME _____ AGE_____

ADDRESS_____

CITY_____ STATE _____ ZIP _____

Please allow four to six weeks for delivery. Offer good in the U.S. only. Sorry, mail orders are not available to residents of Canada. Prices subject to change.

ARE YOU A STRANGER?™

If so, get busy and send us your

Cool Drawings

or

SCARY STORIES

and you may see your work in ...

THE STRANGERS™

NEWSLETTER

Send to your fiends at:
STRANGERS ART & STORIES
Montage Publications
9808 Waples St.
San Diego, California 92121

JOIN THE FORCES!

STRANGERS

An incredible new club exclusively for readers of Strange Matter™

To receive exclusive information on joining this *strange* new organization, simply fill out the slip below and mail to:

STRANGE MATTER™ INFO •Front Line Art Publishing • 9808 Waples St. • San Diego, California 92121